To Yuji
with thanks for your encouragement

Designed by Louise Millar

Printed and bound in Belgium by Proost
for the publishers Piccadilly Press Ltd.,
5 Castle Road, London NW1 8PR

ISBN: 1 85340 641 4 paperback
1 85340 646 5 hardback

5 7 9 10 8 6

Typeset in 22pt Stone Serif

A catalogue record for this book is available from the British Library

Also available in this series:

BABY LEMUR
ISBN: 1 85340 ~~~
1 85340 546 9 (h/b)

BABY TIGER
ISBN: 1 ~~~ 340 504 3 (p/b)
1 85340 509 4 (h/b)

*Susan Hellard is an acclaimed illustrator who lives in North London.
She has illustrated a number of children's books, and is well-known
for bringing to life the character Dilly The Dinosaur.*

Baby Elephant

SUSAN HELLARD

Piccadilly Press • London

Although Ephra was the smallest baby
elephant in the herd, she had the biggest ears.

The trouble was, she didn't use them.
She never listened.

Like when she had her mudbath.
It was such fun wallowing in all
that squishy mud! She didn't
listen to her mother saying,
"That's enough now, Ephra."

And when she went on her favourite walk through the trees, she didn't listen to her aunt saying, "Hurry up, Ephra." So the whole herd had to wait for her to catch up.

When the baby elephants took turns playing under the rainbow waterfall Ephra didn't listen to her father calling, "Time to come out now."

Because of Ephra, some
of the other baby elephants
didn't get a turn.

"Don't stray too far
from the herd, Ephra!"
shouted her grandmother.

But Ephra paid no attention.
She could only think of the
long grass tickling her tummy.
Her grandmother had to run
to catch her and bring her back.

Her mother, her aunt, her father and her grandmother just couldn't make Ephra listen to anything they told her.

But one day
everything changed for Ephra.
After a long, hot walk
the herd reached the edge
of the biggest, bluest lake
Ephra had ever seen . . .

All Ephra could think about was
jumping into the cool water and
swimming to the tiny green
island in the middle.

She didn't listen to the whole herd shouting, "Stay close to the edge! The water is full of dangerous . . ."

"...crocodiles!"

But Ephra had already jumped in!

Suddenly Ephra was surrounded
by snapping teeth. The island
wasn't an island at all but a
group of hungry crocodiles!

But the other elephants had seen Ephra's danger. The whole herd stampeded into the water, scaring the crocodiles away!

Poor Ephra had a badly nipped tail,
but she was safe.

And from then on, Ephra used her big ears to listen to everyone!

Facts About Elephants

There are African elephants and Indian elephants. African elephants have ears shaped like Africa, and Indian elephants have ears shaped like India.

Elephants are the biggest land mammals, and have huge appetites. An African elephant eats about 200 kilos of vegetable matter each day. They eat leaves, fruit, and the bark of trees.

As the seasons change, elephants migrate in search of food and water.

Elephants live in herds of up to ten. They have a female leader whom they follow blindly. The family unit passes on its knowledge – the younger elephants are taught about trails and water holes by the elders.

Baby elephants have a long and carefree childhood, playing, taking baths and learning. The whole herd helps take care of the babies – rather like a giant crèche.

Elephants offer each other mutual aid and show great affection for one another, by making noises and caressing each other with their trunks.

Herds and families joyously converge at water holes. They feast on the plants and fruit and indulge in mudbaths, showers and swimming.